Unfair!

Written by Catherine Baker
Illustrated by Neil Sutherland, Blue-Zoo and Tony Trimmer

It was raining and **U** was getting wet.

U was upset.

A and I had a plan.

a i r, air!

The air was puffing at **u**.

Now U was not wet, but
he was still upset!

h-air, hair!
U got lots of hair.

U got long hair and
a big beard!

The hair got longer and
longer and longer.

P was keen to help.

s-n-i-p, snip!

U had a haircut, but
he was still upset.

Now **U** was sad, but
F had a good plan!

U was feeling a lot better now!
They all had fun at the funfair.